I0745015

ALIOU

A NOVEL OF THE BACKWAY

ERIC REESE

Copyright © 2019 by Eric Reese

All rights reserved.

No part of this book may be reproduced in any form or by any electronic or mechanical means, including information storage and retrieval systems, without written permission from the author, except for the use of brief quotations in a book review.

ISBN: 978-1-925988-26-0

This book is dedicated to all the Alious and Bintous whose bodies have decayed at the bottom of the sea!

Migration gives a blank cheque to put anything you don't feel like addressing in the memory hold. No neighbours can go against the monster narrative of your family.

- JUNOT DIAZ

FOREWORD

We only have two choices – do something or do nothing.

TONY KIRWAN

CONTENTS

1

***

I'M A GAMBIAN

There was something almost magical about the sounds of the birds at dawn. In Gambian villages like this, it was a reminder that even though the darkness had found its way to the village; the sun would always rise again. The birds would always remind you of what it felt like to be alive, to wake up, and to find you have all your limbs still attached to your body. They also would remind you that your family was still in one piece and spread across your compound. The sound of the cock is always a beautiful sound to hear.

Sometimes, families would wake up in the middle of the night to the sound of the bloody cries of war and the heart-breaking sobs of death. Tribal wars were a part that had become almost routine to the Gambian people. Sometimes, a neighbouring village just woken up and raided another village, just because they differed over something petty.

Aliou threw off the threadbare material that served as a blanket. It was time to be up and about, and even though the weather was chilly, he and the other children from neighbouring compounds made their way to the village stream to fetch water that would be used in their separate compounds. The water they would use for their morning bath before they made their way to school.

The school was a few miles away from the small village. The village comprised about twenty compounds, and occasionally you might find over fifty people in a compound. Some were family members from remote villages who had run back to the town after their places of residence had gotten attacked, and others were guests that had been given shelter.

In Aliou's compound, there were about fifty people. He shared a room with ten other boys. Each given a limited spot to declare as his own. Sometimes, the youths spent nights arguing over who wanted or deserved a spot, with the bigger ones bullying the little ones and seizing control of the best sleeping spaces. Unfortunately for Aliou, he was one of the younger boys.

His father had three wives and twelve children.

Growing up in such a huge household was both a blessing and a curse for him. There were good moments and bad ones. Although his father's three wives usually got along, there were still those occasional squabbles to deal with.

Squabbles that turned into something big when care was not taken, or until the neighbours went out to meddle. Sometimes, when such disputes took place, a wife might refuse to feed the other wife's sons if it was her day to cook. As far as she was concerned she controlled the day, and no one could criticise her for what she preferred or preferred not to do when the kitchen was concerned.

Despite the cold wind blowing, the children had no choice but to have their baths from the cold water from the stream. The little ones, like Aliou, would bathe in pairs so that the other ones could take their turns in due time, and bathe before school. Sometimes, when the older ones were feeling rowdy, they would take control of the baths, and the younger ones would have no choice but to bathe outside.

The trip to school was fun, as they went in groups with the children from the other compounds making the journey more entertaining. Sometimes, they would stop by the roadside to play with insects and lizards, until the older ones would chase them away.

On other occasions, they would disappear and skip school for a whole day.

The school was an old building that made the villagers wonder how on God's green earth it was still standing. Its walls had cracks all over, and the paint wasn't even that visible anymore. Children from various villages attended the school and that caused the class to be overcrowded. This encouraged the bigger kids to skip the boring classes and go to nearby farms, to steal mangoes and other fruits till the farmers noticed their presence and chased them away from their farms. Once, Aliou got caught by the owner of a farm where he was stealing fruits. When he tried to run away, he tripped over a rock and ended up with a deep gash on his knee. He received six painful strokes of cane when he was reported to his father.

Aliou's father was a strict man of average stature. Aliou's memories of his dad were mostly of him punishing him for disobeying rules. Occasionally, he praised Aliou for doing well in school. His father hardly ever smiled unless his friends would come around with big business plans or some money-related issues. Because of this, his lips would stretch into twice its size and his yellow teeth would flash for the world to see. It was when Aliou had grown up and looked back that he realised that there were a bunch of things he didn't know about his father.

Although, he knew his father's favourite meal and when his father bought new clothes, Aliou didn't know why he would always buy more brown outfits. He was tall and had a full head of hair. Though Aliou's father was not rich, he had always tried his best to provide for his household. Life was hard, and that was why Aliou wanted to make it big someday.

Only two people in the village had got scholarships to the big institutions in the capital. Aliou's cousin, his father's elder brother's son was one. He remembered the big party that was thrown in the compound that day. There was a bunch of celebration and Aliou had seen his father's brightest smile that day. The best part that day was the meat that was avail− able. Aliou, his cousins, and their friends took more than they could eat, and they all ended up with upset stomachs later that day.

Aliou remembered how he boasted to his friends he too one day will have such a big party thrown, and that there would be more meat than they could ever chew. Little things like that fuelled Aliou's fire to succeed. He was a bright kid and was quick to catch onto whatever the schoolteacher was teaching except there was one problem; getting him to pay attention. His teachers all made countless complaints about him being a restless kid. He was more interested in sports than schoolwork. He was amazing at football, and even the teachers liked seeing him play during physical education classes or break periods. His great football skills earned him the nickname - Aliou Messi, as the villagers believed if luck shone on him and his family, Aliou would grow up to be like the very much popular footballer; Leo Messi. Aliou believed it sincerely, with every bone and fibre in his body.

People looked at him and told him he was destined for greatness. His maternal grandmother, who was eighty-some- thing-years-old, would always tell him that prominence in humans was something that could be recognised at an early age. Aliou, had the semblance of someone who would turn out doing remarkable things. Sometimes, he would reflect and wonder what really happened. Did he somehow change the course of his destiny?

People could do that right? They could wake up one morning and do actions that could alter their destined paths, or at least that was what folk said, especially his Islamic schoolteacher. He was a man was in his mid-thirties, full of life and fantasies. His character was calm, even though sometimes when frustrated with his students, he would change into a demon they couldn't understand, whipping them viciously with his cane. Besides that, his Islamic classes were always engaging. The kids would all make a circle around their teacher, listening to him narrate tales from the Quran as they pictured every word, trying to re-live the reported tales.

But that thrill got pulled away every time, they had to recite the Quran from their wooden slates. And by the time he became ten years old, he had memorised the entire Quran in Arabic. No one cared that he did not understand what every word meant. It was a thing of pride in the village when someone memorised the Quran at such an early age. That was the first time his father had patted him on the back and told him the words that for years he would hold dear to the bottom of his heart.

"I am proud of you."

That was the nicest thing his father had ever said to him, and even later when his stepbrother had become envious, un– leashed his fury, beating Aliou over something silly after his Quranic graduation. It was still worth it, even though his injury leads to his inability to play football for some time. Nothing could take that moment of joy away. Though, this suffering did not leave in vain for long.

His mother had beat his brother senseless too, and

that caused a big fight in the house. His mother had hissed at his stepmother, throwing salt on her wounds by telling her she was only jealous that her son had achieved nothing at the age of fifteen. That had angered the other wife, even more, causing her to launch at his mother. The two women fought like children as the other adults tried to separate them, and all the children stood around and watched in wonderment.

All it took was the powerful voice of Aliou's father to set everything back in order. After listening to both sides to figure out who was wrong, both women were admonished. He pointed out that it was troubling that two grown women be seen fighting amid the compound like a bunch of kids. Overcome by ridicule and anger, his stepmother packed her clothes that evening and headed to her parents' home in a neighbouring village.

It took his father a month of begging and taking fruits to her family before she was persuaded to come back. According to her, he favoured Aliou's mother, his last wife, over them all. She complained that she had three kids and one of them was a male and that she deserved all the affection. After all, she was the first wife and had given him four sons to bear their father's name. Due to custom, Aliou's mother was made to kneel in the middle of the compound to apologise to the first wife as she was the oldest and earned that much consideration. Even at that tender age, Aliou had felt disgusted seeing his mother kneel to the other wife. As a smug smile adorned her face, she was left with a mark on her cheeks was likely to stay forever. It would be many years later that Aliou would realise that it might be an embarrassment to him. But to his mother, it was a badge of honour she wore; being injured while fighting for her child, and it was sufficient for her.

Sometimes, his cousin Daouda, who was studying medicine, in the city, visited home. Aliou could remember the excitements that accompanied his visits. He used to bring those delicious sweets and a lot of stories. At night, mats would be spread in the courtyard, and they would all gather around, sharing stories amongst themselves. During these visits, his cousin was the storyteller. And from then onward, they all felt they needed to see what the city was like, even if it was just for a brief stay. Later in life, Aliou would realise just how much those stories helped him mature. This was a way of getting by for many of them; the fantasy tales they shared satisfied their souls even though most of them knew this was a way of life they may never experience.

Aliou's cousin Daouda was a tall and lanky young fellow, who always laughed at everything. His thundering voice was always eager to share whatever he experienced with the world at large. He loved the attention he received from the villagers. From child-hood, he was one of Aliou's biggest supporters. He would always advise Aliou on what and what not to do and kept advising him to continue practising foot- ball, as it might one day be his ticket to a better life out of the village.

"Let me tell you a secret."

Although Aliou knew that it was no secret, he nevertheless listened. Taking a spiritual observation of each sentence.

"When I read well in school, most people told me I should stop wasting my time and enjoy life, as I could never get out of this village. They insulted me; calling me a jobless bookworm and told me it would be better I remove all those foolish ideas from my head. I was told only then would life become easier." He stopped, with an expression in his eyes that Aliou couldn't figure out.

"What I am trying to say is that, when you are trying to do what you are good at, people will always try to put you down. Do not let them, just look at me now. What do you think would have happened if I had listened to them and let them do so?"

Daouda spoke with an eerie laugh, slapping Aliou on the shoulders. It was something Daouda was fond of, and to him, it was harmless. Others deemed it as unpleasant. But despite how annoying he might get, and the rumours that people shared about him regarding him not being sane in the head, Aliou liked his cousin a lot. Daouda always invited him to hang around and treated him better than the rest. He even gave Aliou candy whenever no one was watching. Once, he brought him a very nice shirt with a picture of Leo Messi. Aliou wore it every day after that until it got stolen.

Aliou was more of an outdoor person, and although he had two sisters from the same mother, he wasn't particularly close to any of them. One was older than him, and the other was much younger. They had a cordial relationship, but that was it. When Aliou looked back on his life, he would have preferred it to be different, he wondered how life would have been if he'd been close with them.

But again, that was the way of life he experienced. His community was a conservative one, and you hardly ever saw siblings from opposite genders have a more than cordial relationship. It was unheard of. When he was twelve, his oldest sister had gotten married to a boy in the neighbouring village, and the only thing he was excited about was the fact that he was able to travel there.

Even though most of the villages in that area had

common norms, they were big differences here and there. He could remember seeing his mother cry so hard when they were about to leave the village. It was a known fact that his mother was close to his sister; Rahamatou. But his mother never hid that he was her favourite. It was later that he would understand that the reason was because he was a male, and having a male son was a thing of honour to a woman in their community, right next to getting married.

His father's second wife had three daughters, and she was treated like an outcast in the house. She and her daughters kept to themselves until it was time for one to get married. Though, the girls in the village went to school, their education was not treated as a priority, and most of them just managed to finish their primary education before being married or forced to get engaged in trade peculiar to women in the community. The eldest daughter had remained unmarried at twenty-five, and that had added to their mother's pain. She was however popular for making one of the best local snacks around the area, but that wasn't enough to keep people's tongues from wagging now and then. Some would say she, like her mother, was cursed, and that was why men found her repulsive. Others said the reason she was not married was that the men from their village were afraid she might have inherited her mother's misfortune and might end up giving birth to only female children too. People loved to gossip.

These were things that Aliou's young mind never took into consideration. It was normal to him; a life he was used to, and he knew no other way of life then. One day, the eldest daughter's body was found in the village stream, floating on the surface. Some had said she had gone to fetch water and had accidentally fallen in. But rumours were making the rounds in the village; saying that the first daughter, in the middle of the night, had snuck out of the house and went to the stream and had taken her own life. No one knew the authenticity of the stories, and those were bad tales that people only whispered to themselves in the darkest hours of the night.

It was considered a taboo and a curse for someone to end his or her own life, no matter how tough life got. And that was why nobody wanted to be caught telling such tales. They did not wish for the misfortune to fall on their own families. After her death, her mother spoke little and did nothing. When Aliou looked back, he remembered that every time he saw her; she had always looked lost a little, like a ghost, and she seemed to be disappearing slowly, blending in with the surrounding wind. Aliou felt his sister's death as she was one of the nicest people to him and the rest of the kids. She had such a good and kind spirit, and that was why many people wondered why she never got married. She would always give out parts of the snacks she sold for free, and when he was much younger, she comforted him whenever he would run off to cry somewhere after he was beaten by the elder ones who would try to bully him into silence. Her name was Rahamatou, and she was a fine girl with a beautiful heart.

It was much later that Aliou would realise that the town had failed him in more ways than one and many others like the sweet, kind Rahamatou. Sometimes, he would still see her face in his dreams, beckoning to him to come rest under a shade with her.

Sometimes, Aliou and some boys in the village looked for small jobs; the most jobs being to help farmers with their work during the harvesting season. And payment came in different forms. Sometimes, they got foodstuff in return, and occasionally, they got money to spend which they preferred. Those were the good times. When Aliou felt generous enough, he would share the money with his mother. However most of the time, he would just spend a little and save the rest of the day; hoping he would get a chance to leave the village one day.

Aliou hated working on the farms, especially his father's. One day, when he had mustered enough courage, he asked his father why he didn't pay them like the rest of his friends. His father had looked him straight in the eye and said "Have you ever paid me for feeding you and clothing you? What about your school fees I pay, do you contribute to that too? If you want me to pay you, then, by all means, get out from my house, remove my blood that flows through your veins, and drop the name and title that proves you are my son. Only then can I pay you for working on my farm."

With another look of anger, disgust, and something he couldn't put the finger on, Aliou made his way back to work, while his siblings snickered behind him. That was one mistake he never made again. Sometimes, when the international football matches were going on, they would all gather in the football clubs (small rented TV rooms) that served as a cinema to the villagers. Sweat from their bodies created a terrible smell as they all jumped and shouted at the activities of the footballers, who could neither hear nor see them. Sometimes when things didn't go well for some teams, supporters would resolve to fighting, to protect the honour of their various football clubs. And that would lead to all of them being chased away from the club by the owners. But apart from those types of moments, watching football with men all over the village was great fun.

Aliou continued to do well in school, even

though most of the time, he was more focused on his football skills. Though if left to him, the football skills would take control, and the school work would be left in the background. Daouda would always warn him against doing that, telling him education was key and football.

"Focus on both equally, Aliou," he often repeated. "If you excel in both, success would be yours."

In fact, he promised him that if he did great in his common entrance examinations, he had a big surprise waiting for him. That was more than enough to keep Aliou going. Aliou was a very determined person, and it was no surprise he did well in whatever he set his mind on. That personality had always been his biggest asset and his worst. It is said, "Too much of anything turns bad."

Life moves in different usual ways in the village; like the occasional cases of politicians going from one village to the other spreading lies and making false promises to win the votes of the people. Most times, they even came with money and foodstuff for the people, and sometimes the youths in the village were hired to help with electoral campaigns.

And then there were the occasional cases of funny incidents. Like that one time that a man was almost torn into pieces by a dog when he had snuck into a certain compound to continue an illicit affair with another man's wife. People said it was fate that had caught up with him, and the incident had become a thing of warning in the village. You would hear parents warning their children with words like:

"If you keep doing bad things, your leg will end up like that of Ahmadou, and you will end up waddling like a duck."

Ahmadou soon moved into town with his family after the incident, because his life in the village became unbearable after that, and the woman he was having an affair with ran away just as soon as that happened. The woman had not been divorced by her husband.

But like everything else in life, things in the village was bound to come and go. And soon after their demise, people started to forget their faces and their stories, as new things happened, that gave people something to talk about. Life was okay for Aliou's household, apart from the general squabbles that took place now and then.

However, things started to go south when there was an outbreak of cholera in the village. Many people; especially kids were lost to the outbreak, including Aliou's younger sister and a few of his cousins. The village took a more sombre atmosphere as most families had lost at least one person to the epidemic. People became afraid, and some wondered if they had upset Allah. It was a belief that all the bad things happening to them was a punishment.

Prayers in the village increased, and people even changed their actions, hoping that it would cause the epidemic to stop and put an end to all the mourning. Aliou's mother took his sister's death quite hard. She stopped eating and started spending entire days locked up in her room, crying her heart out. Soon, she fell terribly ill.

Aliou was scared out of his wits, as at a point, he thought she was dying. Fortunately, she did not although she wanted to. The plague soon ended, however not before many people in their household had their souls taken. At a point in his life, Aliou looked back and wished that he had not been spared during those times; maybe if his life had been taken, then he wouldn't have witnessed the hardships that had later happened to him and his family.

His mother's depression lasted way past the epidemic, but slowly, she started to get over it. At least that was what he thought back then. During those years, he didn't understand that people hardly ever got over things like that, they just learned how to deal with and hide it better. But whatever his mother did, it seemed to have worked for her.

He thought part of the reasons why she soon got over her pain was the knowledge that she wasn't the first, mostly because people wouldn't let her forget that she wasn't. Many told her that she should be lucky that her daughter had died in her arms. Most of the refugees in the village had watched loved ones die cruelly in the hands of stranger's right before their eyes, and there was nothing they could do about it. Sometimes people travelled or went out, only to return to see long trials of blood and the gory bodies of those they left behind. In a village like theirs, people were always willing to remind you of the fact that things could have been far worse.

"You should be lucky," he remembered one villager saying. "Jamilatou's daughter was raped and slaughtered right before her eyes, but she is still walking on two feet and going through life as if nothing happened. Be grateful for the way things ended for your daughter, at least her death was a natural one, no matter the way it came. Many people aren't so lucky."

He saw his mother sitting with her legs outstretched before her, bowing her head as guilt crept into her so visible through the glow in her eyes. The villagers' words would settle in until it registered. She would later realise that many people besides her were struggling to adapt themselves without their lost loved ones.

Aliou wished that she had grown to make sense of

it all and heal. He hoped she, like many others who were not guilt-tripped dealt with the circumstances. Things could have been worse. But that was all they could do now is have faith and prayer.

Remembering the past sometimes, was like seeing your last of the buttermilk in a time of famine spill and get absorbed by the hungry earth determined to absorb anything and not leave a trace behind. You only watch with nothing you can do about it. If you tried to scoop it up, the sand would be more. Your milk was now part of the earth. Forever gone. This was why Aliou hated looking back to the past.

The past was much like the earth itself, it housed the root of all. It pulled you towards it, guiding your decisions. Whatever you do, you rehearsed the story. Just like that, the past would forever stay with him. There were good memories from Aliou's childhood and early teen years in the village. A lot had happened that he wished he could change or forget.

In the village, his life revolved around working on the farm, eating, praying, sleeping, playing football, going to school and Dara (Islamic studies). When he was finished with primary school, things got a little better for his family. His father's produce grew more, and he found himself with a fresh pair of sandals and school uniform. Life was now wonderful.

Whenever life comes to you knocking on the

door with plenty of bouillie, you might be visited by a storm that might shatter every beautiful thing you had if you are not careful. This was why he was so afraid of being cheerful, for he perceived that one day, all might end unexpectedly. For when life comes to take away its gift, it is not bothered whether you are standing on your feet or unprepared.

It will barge into your home without a single warning, snatching away all it has given. Leaving you to drown wallow in the quicksand of self-loathing, as it laughs at you. It was true what his Islamic teacher had said:

"There is always the calm before the storm."

Aliou understood its meaning well. After a series of unfortunate events, he had learned to give up faith in the worldly life he used to cherish so much.

2

"YOU ARE NOT WRONG, SISTER"

If Aliou could trace the day that everything started going downhill, it would have to be after his sister came home due to a bitter divorce from her husband.

The reason was nothing other than she had never had given birth to a child. Aliou didn't understand then it wasn't her fault. He, like many children his age, somehow believed women just magically gave birth and then somehow their prayers come true. If he had known that wasn't the case, he would have at least tried to be more helpful and sympathetic, instead of ignoring her and pretending she wasn't important just like everyone else had treated her.

It was on a hot day; his father and some men were seated under a large hut. It served as a shelter for extracurricular activities like the board games they played. If Aliou's memory served him well, it was on a Friday, after they had all gone to the mosque for Jummat prayers. When they came back, Aliou had gone to help his mother with some chores, and their father and the other elders were playing a game of cards as if forced to do so. All taking large gulps of water from the ceramic pot balanced before them when his sister ran in the compound. Her face was swollen, and she was holding nothing but the bag she had left the house with.

There was a moment of silence as their eyes set on her. Somehow they all recognised, and their father glanced away from her as if she was a ghost. It was like he couldn't see her. She tried to utter a quick greeting, and then she made her way quietly and quickly inside the house. Her heart sank lower and lower, down to her stomach, as she passed all the eyes that were on her.

As soon as her mother saw her, she hurriedly dropped the vegetables she was cutting for dinner and stood up. These days, she did her own personal cooking even when it was not her turn to do the general cooking in the compound. Aliou didn't know whether it was because out of fear of what her co-wives might put inside her food as that was common where she was, or she preferred eating her own self-made dishes. Either way, it was ok with Aliou, as he loved eating her meals.

His mother let out a loud cry before slumping down on the floor, with her legs outstretched before her. Something Aliou had seen many times and learned that it was an expression of sorrow for many women in the village.

"They have killed me. They have done it," she cried uncontrollably, while his sister moved closer to her before she attempted to calm her down.

However, as soon as her hands touched her, she moved away, still mumbling words of blame under her breath. At that moment, one would have guessed his sister murdered someone. But in their village, a dead marriage was just as bad. The stigma that occurred with divorce was almost heart- breaking to observe. Nobody even wished to find out her side of the story. Everyone assumed it was the daughter's fault because no matter what went on, she should have stayed; they would always say. Some even declared she was a selfish person for spoiling her marriage saying that the husband still stayed with her even though she was barren.

Aliou blamed her then too, and for his mother's depression. Right after tongues wagged in the village, he later realised how harmful their actions were. Maybe there was the possibility that his sister was not at fault as the man's other wife was just as barren as his sister. He had heard men too could become impotent in their later years although he didn't take this opinion seriously. It was an area no one dared considered especially growing up in the village. Like any other thing in life, it passed on. With time, people forgot, as new events happened day after day. There was a man who lived a few compounds away from them. He was accused of raping and impregnating his cousin's niece, who was under his guardianship. It was common in the village that out of respect for a person; a father may give out his child to be raised by another man as his own.

Unfortunately, in this case, it was a huge mistake.

The man and his relatives were chased out of the village due to threats from the little girl's family. There was an opinion that the man confessed his mistake and he was sorry although he kept saying that the girl was the one who kept tempting him. She was thirteen and was innocent enough that the man's story was unbelievable. The girl's father took a knife one night and went to attack the man vowing to destroy him and his entire generation. Once he arrived, the neighbours intervened, and the matter was taken up by the village head who had the final say.

The tongues of the villager's wagged so hard that Aliou was surprised they didn't fall off. After a few months, the news died down. Months later, the little girl had complications with the pregnancy and had died afterward. Tongues of the villagers arose to wag again; many rumouring it was the work of the first wife. An old village woman even claimed she had seen her at the Witchdoctor's hut. What she was doing there by herself, nobody knew. The villagers were so excited about having something to talk about that they didn't even care. At last, there was someone to blame, and that was all that mattered.

ALIOU BETTER FOCUS

Aliou's juvenile years were more concentrated on football and the promise his cousin Daouda had made to him. Daouda had vowed to take Aliou with him to the big city, to continue his education, under the condition that he would study hard and pass his exams. This was the only motivation Aliou needed to pay more attention to his studies. His seriousness made his mother smile every time she saw him reading. Pride gleamed in her eyes. Every time she smiled at him like that, her sorrow seemed to disappear. Sometimes, he would attempt to teach her how to read.

She would laugh bashfully and say, "What this brain of mine can take and if it can even understand what is going on. What use would it be to me? Just go and read it and become a great man just like your cousin." Regularly, she would stop and say to herself. "My son, my own son will be a great man from this place."

Aliou would smile at her with much enthusiasm. After one or two lessons, he stopped trying to teach her how to read and felt that it was of no purpose anymore. His sister, however, showed an interest in his textbooks. Since she had a primary school level of education, he would usually find her with his books in her room. Inside of them were hinted she kept writing here and there. Aliou later asked if she would like extra lessons and she cheerfully agreed. He knew that it was what she was hoping for. However, they both kept it a secret from the rest of the family, as they knew that they would make fun.

One day, in the middle of a conversation, she had suggested that it would be great if she could go back to school since she basically did nothing at home besides helping her mother and co-wives with house-work. Her mother's face had wrinkled as if she had seen a ghost, and she had responded in an even more disgusted tone when she heard the rumour.

"School? What do you need school for? Instead of you focusing on finding yourself a husband, you're thinking about school." Aliou saw the pain in his sister's eyes at their mother's statement and very much broke his heart when their mother added:

"That's if you can even manage to keep one."

He had tried then to come to his sister's defence. "But mother, she only works at home. She can work and go to school too."

"I can see that you will not understand that she cannot. You are a man. Where in your life have you seen a woman in this village or anywhere study up to the level you are at now? Huh! A husband is the best option for her now before it's too late."

"But mother," Aliou argued. "Brother Daouda told me that there are a bunch of educated girls in the city. In fact, he said that he once almost was served to by a female doctor. She can still go to school while being married."

"Daouda? What does Daouda know?" his mother replied.

If the situation had been a little less serious, he would have chuckled at it all. His mother usually complimented his cousin as the most brilliant young man in the village.

"And you continue talking about the city; don't you know how the girls are there? Why will you want your sister to become like them? They are rude and loose. Once, Aunty Maryamou was telling me, she saw one of those girls wearing trousers. Men's cloth-ing! What kind of respectable woman wears trousers?"

Aliou gave up arguing, but his mother did not;

complaining about the city girls and how immoral they all were to her, attributing most of it on the education they had, and making references to some things Aunty Maryamou told her. It was hilarious how she kept believing Aunty Maryamou. Mom even said once that Aunty was such a pathological liar that the only thing she would take from her was her confession that Allah was one.

Aliou and his sister never brought up the matter again but continued their lessons in private. She was remarkably smart and always made sure to ask questions. In a little time, her English conversation skills improved incredibly. He wondered what kind of progress she would have made if she was tutored by a real teacher.

The exam season began, and the village boys were all a bit tense: writing their junior secondary school examinations. The thing that had scared them the most was the fact that major invigilators were to be brought in from the capital. Some people said the invigilators were so good that they could fish you out for just speculating about cheating. Once, a boy was caught with a piece of paper during the exam, and the invigilators went away with him to the capital, and no− body heard of him ever since.

All the evening football matches came to a halt and were taken over by extra practices and tutorials in the evenings, with Aliou heading some of them. Even the parents tiptoed around the houses when the lessons were going on in the chosen home as the children had their lessons in turns. Whoever's turn it was, was responsible for hosting the group. Some students even dropped out weeks before the exam believing, they would be better off as farmers like their fathers. The chores for the boys were dropped as well due to the lessons. Aliou loved it.

The day the exam started, the whole village was filled with whispers from here and there. People were whispering as if they too would be taken away to the capital if they were caught talking out loud. The invigilators looked frightening, and the head one was a white man. Sure, the villagers had seen white men sometimes, but most were missionaries trying to sell something. The man's English seemed difficult to understand and sounded like a hot yam in his mouth when he spoke. He was the first person to address the students in their very neat uniforms, which was not a sight that was seen every day in the community.

"You all must know that cheating is a dreadful crime and anyone who is caught cheating shall be expelled from the school and disqualified from writing his exams." His tone was authoritative, and although the students may not have fully understood what he was saying, the word was reached definitively.

The exam lasted for two weeks. When it was all over, the white man and his entourage packed all they came with along with the students' papers and went back to wherever they had come from. Aliou was scared that maybe he didn't do well because of the tight security and the fear made him nervous throughout the exam period. Sometimes, it took a second or third reading for him to understand the questions. His mother's prayers for him had doubled, and even his father gave him anxious glances whenever he passed by.

It was during the exams that Aliou had his first crush on a girl named Bintou. Her family moved to the village from a neighbouring one about two years ago. She was remarkably pretty with large black eyes and a petite figure. Though she was shy, there was something strong about her personality and the way she carried herself. Aliou was mesmerised by the girl, and he would always stammer whenever she was in proximity. If his friends caught him staring at her, they made fun of him by saying: "Aliou loves Bintou."Bintou for some odd reason was drawn to his sister although there was a five-year age gap. After a few days, she started coming to Aliou's compound more often. Whenever he sat in the front, he would hear them whispering and laughing over something.

"What are they talking about?" he often

wondered while he daydreamed about destiny with Bintou.

She would let out a melodious sound whenever Aliou passed by while she and Aliou's sister were studying. Due to religious and cultural reasons, Bintou and Aliou hardly ever spoke after giving the traditional greetings. The occasional smiles and glances they threw at each other were secretly transmitted when they knew no one was watching them. One day, his dreams came true as his sister approached him with a deal he couldn't refuse. She explained that the reason Bintou had been coming around more often was because she needed more advanced lessons.

"Would you like to help, Aliou?" she asked.

He couldn't refuse her offer. Although he tried to play it cool, his heart was bursting with joy. The sarcastic look on his sister's face after his response signalled that she already knew what Aliou was planning inside of his head. Perhaps there were greater things to come.

4

"YES, MY BOY DID IT"

At the beginning of their secret classes, it was difficult for both Bintou and Aliou. But slowly, they began to get over their awkwardness and had become good friends. Three months after tutoring Bintou and studying for his own schoolwork, Aliou's school results were posted, and an excited boy came to narrate the information. A sense of fear and excitement gripped Aliou's heart, reverently playing that this result would do nothing but favour him. If it did not, not only would it ruin his chance of leaving the village, it would also disappoint his parents, and perhaps make him lose the little chance he had with Bintou. How would he look her in the eye and then tell her he had failed when he was tutoring her?

His legs shook a little as he rushed to the school;

he learned by now, news must have already spread the results. A crowd of boys was gathered around the notice board. He saw a woman standing there, out of place in the mist of young students. She pushed her way through the crowd while her hands were on the shoulder of another boy. Even without seeing the boy's face, Aliou recognised it was Osman. This boy was so stuck to his mother he couldn't do anything without her. The kids had given him the nickname 'woman wrapper' in their language, because of that. But no matter how much they teased him, he never seemed to care, and would always run to his mother for everything.

If the stories told by the villagers was true, Osman's mother had had miscarriages for ten years, and when she had almost given up hope, she had gotten pregnant with him. Two days later, his father was killed on his way back from a journey. He had been caught up in a tribal war. It was just she and him after that. Some said she locked herself in a room with the boy for about a week and no one knew what she ate or what she fed him. Though the story had different versions, the one thing all the villagers agreed on was that her son was the only thing that kept her from running mad. It was also said he was her anchor during all the dark days of her life.

Aliou joined the struggle, pushing his way through the crowd and not losing his spirit, even after he had been elbowed and pushed back a few times. When he reached the front, or at least as far as he could get, he was shocked to see his name at the top. And before he knew it, the boys turned to his still frame, patting him on the back and shoulders and congratulating him. He couldn't believe he was the overall best in their school. He thought he might at least pass. But even though he knew he had always been topping the class, he had a few competitors who he was sure studied more than him so being the first seemed a little farfetched then, and he refused to even make it an option, so he would not feel disappointed when things didn't go as planned.

He took a few minutes to come out of his mode, and he laughed hard as he shook hands with the boys who extended their hands to him. With great difficulty, he found his way out of the crowd that had blocked his path. He almost ran, and when he considered sprinting back home, he was stopped by the principal and his maths teacher.

"Congratulations. The school is proud of you. Your result brings you to be among the top three in the state, and that is why the education board has awarded you and three others a scholarship to study in the city. However, the school is not a boarding school so find someone to stay with as the scholarship covers only your tuition fees, school uniform, and stationeries."

The principal started, beaming at him. He could count the number of times he had ever seen the principal smile and knowing the smile was directed at him made him feel all giddy on the inside. He couldn't believe this was happening to him. It almost seemed too real to be true.

"Ye... Yes... Yes, sir." he stammered.

Lost for words, and he couldn't think of what else to say. A scholarship? He could not wait for the principal to finish his speech, so he could run home to share the good news with everyone although he knew the news have reached them already . His mates were staring at him even though he knew they were too far to hear what they were saying. He knew they were just waiting for the principal to leave so they could attack him and demand for answers.

"Since your cousin, Daouda is there already, I don't think that will be a problem. Tell your father I will come visit him later at night to discuss the full details with him," Aliou could only nod his head. He felt his mouth dry. He knew he couldn't think of anything to say.

"Congratulations once again (boy)! The madrasa (school) is proud of you. You now have the highest score ever out of the madrasa. Not even your cousin Daouda got that score. Keep working hard, and the world will someday be in your pock− et." His math teacher; a tall, lanky man, who was always properly dressed in a suit with no tie. The students were fond of mocking his European dressing behind his back. They said he looked like a goat ready to be killed for Christmas because of his suit. They couldn't understand why he would suffocate himself in those Westerners' clothes.

"Thank you very much, sirs." Aliou thanked them.

The mudeer (principal) extended his hands and Aliou seemed to lose control of his body. Still, his hand seemed to have a mind of its own as it shook hands with the principal and the math teacher. The rest of the students stared on with their bottom jaw hanging. The only time a student was seen shaking hands with the principal had been when the principal was giving out prizes at the end of the year.

The mudeer (principal) walked away, and the rest of the students jumped at him with a billion questions.

"How did you do it? What was he telling you?"

someone asked and before he could answer, another one asked:

"What was his hand like?"

The questions kept coming: "Was it sweaty? Is it tough like ours?"

They seemed more interested in what the hand-shake was like than what he was told. When Aliou answered their questions, they screamed like they did whenever their favourite football teams won a match. An indescribable feeling of euphoria filled Aliou. He was the centre of attention.

But as always and as expected, there was always someone who has been a success story and wasn't happy with whoever stole the spotlight.

"You are all hailing him as if he is the first boy in this village to get a scholarship."

A spiteful voice said from the back. They all turned and saw Alagie; Aliou's biggest rival.

"He might not be the first, but he got the highest score in this village. No one has ever gotten that score before." A friend defended him, giving Alagie a mean look.

"Shut up, Alagie. You are just jealous because you didn't get the highest score. If you have nothing to say good, just keep quiet." Another student retorted, following it with a loud hiss. Soon, all the boys all threw in their various comments, and it turned into a verbal fight, with Alagie and his friends calling them all sort of names and insulting them and their ancestors. Soon enough, everybody ignored them and left them to their petty comments. That seemed to have worked because people stopped paying them any attention, they realised that they simply wasted their breaths and left the gathering.

Aliou's heart warmed at the way his friends had stood up for him. Soon enough, that feeling was replaced by regret when he remembered that he didn't even bother to ask about their scores. He was too busy being the man of the moment. Most of his friends got in; it seemed Alagie was second on the list, followed by Osman, who had returned home with his ecstatic mother. Some boys made jokes about how Osman would survive if at all, gets enough money to continue his education, and they all laughed.

After spending a few more minutes with his friends and well-wishers, Aliou could finally sprint back home to share the news. As he entered his father's compound, he knew the news had already reached home from the congratulations he received on the way home. A shout of joy was released as the crowd saw him. Everyone wanted to touch him and congratulate him. His mother was weeping in a corner which he learned were tears of joy. His sister was grinning, accepting congratulations on his behalf. Everyone was smiling, and to his greatest surprise even the first wife was grinning and congratulating him. She was usually the grumpiest and meanest person in the compound. But as he learned later in life, many people are attracted to success, and all would be wiped away if they discovered that they could benefit from you. He had earned himself a great name and title in the village, and that was enough reason for her to drop her hatred aside for the moment and embrace the goodness that would come from him to her and her kids.

His eyes scanned the crowd, looking for Bintou and as soon as his eyes locked with hers, they shared a smile oblivious to the rest of the crowd. Apart from his sister, she seemed to always be watching them like a hawk, but she wasn't as discreet as she believed herself to be. It took time before the crowds slowly reduced. Everyone going his or her own way to continue with whatever they were doing earlier promising to come back for the celebration. His father promised it would take place later in the evening. He ordered the young boys to go slaughter his biggest goat so that the women could prepare the food. Everyone rushed to start their duty, with the little ones helping the women gather small pieces of wood so that the fire could be made. Aliou never thought there would be a time in his life when he would be the source of joy for the village. He longed for the lingering people to go away.

"I need to meet with Bintou," he said to himself.

While no one was around, he rehearsed how he would play it cool when he saw her. However for him, meeting with Bintou had to be later when the guests had departed. As disappointed as he was, the secret glances they split was convincing. The house became crowded at night as well- wishers and pretenders came to attend the ceremony. His father chatted with his guests, bragging about his son's achievements with the guests. "The mudeer (school principal) came and met me right here in this compound. He begged me to allow my boy to go to the big school in the capital." He exaggerated the facts as the other men listened in awe, envious but still happy.

"May Allah bless their education they will get! May they become a source of pride for us! Ameen!" One man praised, and there was a chorus of 'Ameen' before the conversation shifted to other directions, and the guests' booming laughter filled the night.

Aliou's mother dressed in her best clothes. Decorated and beautiful, she made her way around, making sure the guests had food, and looking for opportunities to brag. She was gracious for the opportunity to show them she could also produce something great, knowing what the villagers said behind her back. Most had mocked her for having only one male child and being the mother of a divorced woman. Allah had shown them that even one son can become a blessing.

She, a daughter of a poor farmer, was now a reason for the village to smile. Who would have thought? She was in too happy a mood to let anything ruin it. The snide remarks some threw at her bounced off her skin, not affecting her.

His sister and Bintou were also no exception, they all dressed up in their best-looking attires as if they were about to attend a naming ceremony. Aliou shook so many hands that night that his hand felt as if they would fall off. His mouth had gone dry from saying thank you so much. After a while, he slipped away. Sensing the opportunity, his sister sent Bintou to take a cup of the local drink made for the celebration. Although they couldn't talk for a long time, she congratulated him.

The celebrations went late into the night, and by the time the guests dispersed, they were all too tired to clean up. They left the house as dirty as it was.

Aliou slept soundly that night, and he dreamt of Bintou. In his dream, she was wearing a blue dress and holding their daughter in the biggest compound, he had ever seen. At that moment, he could not imagine a future brighter than this.

5

"I'LL MISS YOU BINTOU"

The next day, during a stressful morning of cleaning up the compound, Aliou spent some time alone with Bintou; due to his sister's perfect plan. Everything he had rehearsed seemed to fly out of his head after setting his eyes on her. He could not even remain calm as his body kept betraying him as he kept stuttering. Bintou seemed to have developed some kind of superpower because she was the one leading the conversation. "So, I heard they gave you a house in the city?"

"A house?" He laughed. Realisation dawning on him that the people must have twisted the facts." I am staying with my cousin in his flat. The scholarship does not cover accommodation." He explained to her, finally steadying his voice.

"Oh! I must have misunderstood," Bintou said.

There was a comfortable silence. Each lost to his or her own thoughts. Their eyes moved around the room, moving from the bed to the bag of clothes at the far end corner, and sometimes even landing on the old and faded mat that graced the floor. Aliou was thinking about how things would change for his family if he were a rich man. He would rebuild their whole compound and then marry Bintou and they would stay anywhere they wanted in the world. Maybe France? Their children would look all pure and sophisticated. Whatever happened, they would not be raised in the village. As much as Aliou loved it there, he wanted a different life for them.

"So, if you go. Is that it?" Bintou asked sadly, hoping that he would say no.

"They will give us days off. So, I think I will come back a few times a year." She nodded her head, trying to hide her joy but her mouth kept betraying her with involuntary smiles she couldn't seem to control.

They talked about little things, jumping from topic to topic, and he promised to write her every month. Aliou guaranteed her she too one day would get into a school like his. At first, she did not believe him, but he convinced her as he told her stories of the young girls that made it to the institution he heard of from his crazy auntie. When Aliou told Bintou about the female doctor, she was amazed. A ray of hope it was. Her expression kept encouraging him to talk and he could except that they were inside his father's compound.

When she stood to leave, he stood up too and gave her an awkward hug and a peck on the cheeks. It was something he had read in a book. Bintou froze before rushing out of the room, leaving him standing there just as surprised as she was. His sister stepped in the right after her and gave him a suspicious look.

"What did you do to her?" she demanded.

"Nothing." he lied but she didn't believe him.

"Don't make me regret giving you this opportunity. She rushed out of this room looking flustered. "You'd better be careful."

She warned before he excused himself and left her in the room to finish cleaning. Quite surprised, but also unrepentant about the thing that had happened. The days moved quicker than everyone expected. The time had come when Aliou would be travelling, Some well-wishers brought food stuff, dalasis, and other items for his trip. His cousin, Daouda came to escort him while a distant relative offered to take his belongings to the car garage on his bicycle.

His goodbyes to his family especially his mother was a tearful one. In his sister's room, Bintou burst into tears in the middle of a conversation and he had to comfort her by telling her, he was not far away.

After saying this, she calmed down and was the first to hug him. She darted away embarrassed as the family watched in sorrow. Aliou's mother released her own ocean of tears. She cried so hard that one would think she had received news of his death instead. Right there, his sister snapped at her, telling her he was travelling to the city and not to the heavens.

"He will come back Ummi (mother). Please stop crying!"

She didn't appreciate the comment, but it reduced her tears. The members of the compound began reciting supplications for Aliou; seeking protection against Shaytaan (the devil) and everything that would seek to harm him in the big city. His father shook his hand and patted him on the back. He then handed him a few thousand dalasis and sent him away with prayers. The stepmothers each gave him food items and prayed for him. Before he departed, his mother warned him to be careful before touching anything anyone had given him.

"Be wise, my son. You don't know what might have been put in there. Nowadays, people cannot be trusted."

Aliou said 'yes' to everything she said in agreement.

She then recited another series of prayers and

rubbed over him with her hands. "May Allah be with you."

The journey to the capital was longer than expected. He became tired of watching the road as they passed by the town after town. His body drifted between sleep and consciousness. At a point, he tried to stand up realising it was a car not a bus. A few hours later, the car stopped at a small village for rest and food. It was smaller but more sophisticated than his town. After a couple hours of travelling and the random stops for rest, the passengers reached their destination in one piece.

When they reached at a car park, Aliou took a taxi to Daouda's house. He passed by many fancy places and expected that his cousin's place would be the same. The driver kept going further until they reached another neighbourhood that did not resemble what Aliou saw a few minutes earlier. In fact, their village was far better looking than this place. A terrible smell entered the car window which stank like a mixture of urine, sweat, and rotten food.

"Close the windows!" the driver yelled.

Aliou was at a loss for words and too tired to say anything. He just did what the driver told him. A few miles later, the taxi stopped in front of an old house in basically the same neighbourhood. A group of boys was seated on a wooden bench in front of the house playing a game of cards. Aliou stepped out of the taxi, and they gave him a suspicious look. When they saw Daouda come outside to negotiate payment with the taxi driver, they realised it was his family.

The boys called each other weird nicknames, and Daouda introduced Aliou to them. They seemed friendly, but Aliou still felt tense.

"Why did Daouda tell me to come to this neighbourhood? Is he here visiting his friends?"

All thoughts that ran through Aliou's mind as they breathed in the bad odour of that place. Daouda led him deep through the house, passing a series of rooms and a group of occupants who were mostly women. It turned out that Aunty Maryamou was speaking the truth when she said the women in the city wore trousers. Aliou saw one lady wearing a pair of trousers that only stopped on her thighs. He was shocked and didn't know whether to stare or look away.

What surprised him the most was she was smoking a cigarette. He kept peeking at Daouda, but he seemed unfazed. Aliou can only swallow his comments for later. Finally, they reached a door like the rest but further in the back. Daouda pulled a key from his pocket and opened it.

They walked into a small room that even their rooms back home were bigger than. There were clothes scattered here and there, and his cousin picked them up throwing them in a corner where another pile laid.

"Make yourself at home. You can put your bags right over there." His cousin pointed to an empty corner.

Aliou lay on the bed and fell asleep. His cousin came back almost an hour later with a nylon bag stuffed with food. After they had eaten, they both sprawled on the other mattress in the room.

"So, when are we going home to your place?" Aliou dared to ask after pondering how for a long time.

"Home..." Daouda repeated before letting out a long laugh, leaving the young boy even more confused. "This is home, my boy. Soon you will understand. But for now, you had better rest," he said, turning his back to Aliou, and laughing. Aliou lay on the other side, wondering what was so funny, and most of all trying to make sense of it all.

6

"DAOUDA'S BEEN LYING"

The next day after morning prayers, Aliou made sense of it all. He learned that his cousin was not even studying at all. Daouda was doing odd jobs to survive.

"You don't know what it was like. I came here with big dreams like yours. I was smart, but this place is cruel. No one could support me to finish my studies, and there are a lot of high expectations for me back home. I couldn't let anyone down. Since after my father's death, I am the one everyone looks up to for support. I couldn't bring myself to go back home and tell them I was living a wretched life in this terrible city," Daouda told Aliou later that day. Aliou only half understood what Daouda meant.

"But you. I hope you never end up like me. You

have a bright future ahead. Much brighter than mine. Perhaps you will be the one who will make our family proud."

Aliou hoped that at least school would be everything he expected and not something like the disappointment that his cousin's place was. There were always guys in the house walking back and forth past the room with women. Aliou always felt stupid when they spoke to his cousin. They spoke in street slang and seemed to always talk about how many ladies and drinks they had the prior evening.

Aliou's first day of school was encouraging. The school building was large and decorated in the best part of the town. The school's secretary and principal talked to groups of students as they toured the school on the first day. Aliou felt out of place, and the looks he received from most of the students did not help at all.

When the teacher asked him to introduce himself, he was nervous but willed himself to appear confident. He had to prove them all wrong and show them that a village boy could hold his own. When it was time for the break, most of the students went their way with their colleagues, leaving him to sit alone. Halfway through recess, a boy walked over to him, introduced himself as Yusuf, and they talked. Yusuf was a gentle boy that had a deep voice for his age.

Aliou knew if it wasn't for the scholarship, there was no way he could ever afford to be in a school like this. For what it was worth, he was determined to work hard and come out on top. Deep inside, he still wished he was back home at the village; listening to his sister hum her way around the kitchen, eating his mother's delicious meals, and having secret lessons with Bintou. He missed the village and the life he left behind.

Time went by, and before he knew it, Aliou made a few friends and slowly adapted. As promised, he wrote a letter to Bintou every month. In the letters, he told her how the school and the students were, and how he wished she was there with him. Aliou told her a lot about the girls in his class, girls that resembled her.

"Work hard, for one day, you too would get the same opportunity," he wrote in every letter.

One thing he didn't mention was about was his cousin Daouda's condition. It was best leaving him to remain the hero the villagers thought him to be. As the weeks passed by, Aliou understood Daouda better, and why he had to lie to the villagers when- ever he came there. The city was not as great as they all imag-ined and bragged about. Life was fast, and everyone was looking for money unlike back in the village. He hoped that maybe one day, the city folks will learn to be kind as the people back home.

7

"WHAT IS HAPPENING AROUND ME?"

Somehow, things were not all ponies and unicorns at school. His strong determination to succeed made him many friends and many enemies. He longed for the end of the term so he could return home. However, time took longer. Life in the city differed from what he was used to. People in the city did not seem to care about one other, and they always found reasons to gossip about everything. As much as he hated the way the villagers were so conservative, he couldn't escape the fact that at least most of the city people wanted to see changes.

During weekends, Aliou helped his cousin do odd jobs, and received a share of the wages. Daouda advised him to save as much as possible, so Aliou removed a little from it for his transport to school and lunch break. At times, Daouda was kind enough to give him some of his own money, and before Aliou knew it, he had saved quite a lot.

He decided that when it was time to go back home, he would use the money to buy the family bags of rice and other foods. He would buy materials and books for Bintou and his sister, a new shirt for his father, and gifts for the rest of the house and his friends. All he was waiting for was for the holidays to come. Aliou could not wait.

The Eid break was approaching, and Aliou was excited about going back to see his family. He didn't realise how much he missed home until the night before he was ready to travel back. His body and mind were so restless and anxious that he couldn't even sleep that night. He kept tossing and turning on his bed, waiting for dawn to break.

The call for prayer was sounded, they prayed and then rushed to the bus station. For Aliou and Daouda, they board– ed the first vehicle leaving. There were about six or seven in the car, squeezed inside like animals being taken to the market for sale. Aliou minded none of it, he was just grateful to go back home.

After hours of drowning in heat, they reached their destination. Aliou almost sprinted back home, causing his cousin to laugh. Daouda told him he would get used to not being at home when they first went to the city, but he didn't get it. How could someone get used to not being in a place he had stayed his entire life?

There was a lot of excitement following their arrival, like it before when Daouda came back to the village. In fact, Daouda once confessed to him it was one reason he loved staying for a long time. And it was true.

Aliou's mother was the happiest of them all. She kept asking him about school, life, and if Daouda was treating him well. Aliou told her most truths and lied about living a luxurious life back in the city. Daouda nodded in thanks.

He met Bintou the next day, and she was so appreciative of his gifts. The way she examined what she was given made him feel like finding every good thing in the world to give to her. They spent a long time catching up, and she listened to everything he said with great fascination. Aliou wanted her to see all the things he had told her about first hand.

"I heard the people in the city are nice, is it true?" she asked.

He hesitated in answering and felt that telling her about his bad experiences would ruin the great image she had of the city. He remembered what it felt like; holding those good memories close to him. It was his motivation; the knowledge was like having heaven waiting for you. It was a beautiful thing to hold on to.

"Yes, they are nice. A lot of them are."

She smiled, and he told her about his new friends in the city, the good times they always had, and all the nice things they did for him. By the time he finished talking, Bintou was convinced that it was the nicest and kindness place on earth. He felt a little bad lying to her like that, but the smile on her face convinced him it was worth it.

"By the way, I heard the women are pretty too." Bintou asked innocently. Aliou felt she meant it to be a trick question. He smiled before saying. "Well, they are," Bintou's face fell for a second. "But not as pretty as you." Aliou watched her covering her smile after his comment.

"You are just teasing me," she said.

"No, I am serious. You are prettier than them. Some people are only beautiful on the outside, but few are both, and you are the best."

Aliou meant every word, recognising some of his experiences with a few girls in his new school. Most looked at him as the scum under their shoe and didn't hesitate to make village jokes whenever they saw him. Others were disinterested. They were good ones who didn't care where he was from.

He spent almost a month in the village, meeting his friends, playing football, helping his family and talking to Bintou if they were alone. His cousin left the village after two days because he had to return to work. However, he promised Aliou to come for him at the end of his vacation and take him back to the city. Daouda fulfilled his promise as usual.

Leaving home was a painful experience as Aliou pondered why his village didn't have a secondary school. Since he already experienced living in the city, he knew he really belonged at home. His separation from Bintou would be heart-breaking now that he had more lessons to offer her.

The day that Aliou left, everyone was distraught as if it was his last time visiting. Even his father was sad to see him go. Family members walked Aliou to the front of the compound to board the taxi with Daouda to go to the bus station. They made supplications for them and told them to not to forget Allah ever.

Aliou and Daouda said, "Ameen" and pulled off.

Back in the city, things were back to normal. In Aliou's school, his classroom won the best and neatest class of the month. His marks were excellent, and he was becoming one of the best students in the school.

Aliou's initial reaction to the principal of the school was he was a nice man. However, as the year went on, Aliou saw another side of him which differed from his former principal back home. The new principal's sincerity was questionable. He always treated the rich kids better, and if the parents asked him to help their children by changing the marks, he would do it even if it meant firing the teacher.

A month passed by and Aliou got so caught up with work and school he forgot to write Bintou. She was furious at first, thinking he had betrayed her.He explained and explaining and apologised, and she calmed down and didn't writing him first from now on. Bintou's letters were soothing and always the refresher he needs in the city environment that was suffocating him little by little. Bintou always had interesting stories from the village. She wrote about who gave birth, who got married, who got a divorce, and those that did something ridiculous. Aliou joked and told her she would be a good news broadcaster.

It was from Bintou he learned that his friend Osman had gotten admission into a secondary school in another city. She had told him that Osman's mother had sold almost all her animals for his studies. Most people told her that what she was doing was stupid, but she refused to listen to them as usual. Aliou admired Osman's mother, she was one woman that refused to be moulded by the village and its views. She always stood for what she believed in even if no one agreed with her. And that was why most parents didn't want their boys hanging around with Osman. They claimed he learned bad things from his mother, which would all somehow rub off on their children. Aliou's mother would always tell him to stay away from Osman. However, what most of the people didn't know was that Osman and his mother were opposites.

Aliou dared not to explain that to his mother knowing she would start a long lecture about how kids always turned out to be like their parents. She was convinced Osman was a bad influence. For this reason, Osman often kept to himself and was never bothered with people from the village, apart from a few friends and his mother.

Aliou had a special box in his cousin's room where he kept Bintou's letters. Sometimes, when he was feeling a little blue, he would take out the letters and read them all over again. When replying to her messages, he made it a habit of writing a new phenomenon or anything he had learnt, just in case he forgot to tell her whenever he went back home.

Yusuf, who had become a good friend of his at school, told Aliou that he was madly in love with Bintou and was a hope less romantic; teasing him about the letters, Aliou held on to so dearly. Aliou just played it cool. From what he had read about love, he wasn't so sure about what Yusuf was always saying.

"Look at it this way; even though you hardly see her, you talk about Bintou all the time. You are always writing and daydreaming about her. I am sure you can't sleep most of the nights due to your infatuation. That's what love means." Yusuf expressed.

These words blew Aliou's mind and made him write more letters to Bintou; confessing his love. Yusuf was always nonchalant. Sometimes, he would talk with so much maturity and wisdom that would make one wonder if he was a man living in a boy's body.

Once before, Aliou admitted he loved Bintou, Yusuf had challenged him to ask out a girl who seemed to love him in class. This was after he had learned what the meaning of word "date." The classes in the city weren't segregated as the village. After Yusuf's persistence, Aliou mustered enough courage to do so, and surprisingly, the girl agreed. On their first date, Aliou kept making references to Bintou.

First, it was her laugh, and then the way the girl spoke. In the end, the girl wasn't interested after Aliou told her where he lived.

After the date, the girl stopped speaking to him; only for Aliou to tell Yusuf 'I told you so' and a giggle from the other youngsters in class. Turns out, it was all a plot to find out his true affection for Bintou, and it was wrong to use the girl like that. Aliou apologised a few days later. The girl went out with another boy in class and Aliou was happy for her.

Bintou found out and was not happy about it. Aliou told her everything in a letter, and she refused to reply to any of his letters for a couple of months. He kept apologising in every note he sent. The latest reply he received was a warning never to repeat anything like that again. It took time before things went back to normal. Occasionally, she still asked about the girl. Aliou knew Bintou would never trust him like before.

Aliou got used to the city and even started liking living there. Once he learned its ways, he realised that it was not as bad as he thought. His city friends were more adventuresome, taking him to new places to explore. The main thing that Aliou missed about the village life was the food. The foodstuff there was natural which made the soups tastier.

In the city, he had learned how to cook. Never did he think it would be necessary to learn. Cooking in the eyes of villagers was a unique power only a woman was born with. But in the city, if he wanted to eat, he would have to cook to save money. Aliou became great at the whole cooking thing. When he told Bintou about his newly found interest, she wrote him telling him to stop being silly. She believed he was joking around.

He wished there was a way to bring Bintou with him. The only way that that would happen if they were to wed. Back home in the village, marriage was easy. Young boys and girls got married early all the time. In fact, Aliou had a few companions that were married at sixteen years of age. The thought of marriage would be much more challenging in the capital where he and Daouda could hardly support themselves. If he were to marry, he would have to find a full- time job, leave school and find another place to live.

Aliou thought about the possibilities of losing Bintou often. It scared him senseless. What if one day her parents found her a spouse and wed her off before he discovered? What if Bintou found another man she liked? His worst fears were confirmed soon enough when Bintou sent him a letter around the middle of the month which was rare.

———————

The letter was a tragic one. Her parents had spoken about marrying her off, and Bintou had run out of all the ways to avoid them and their intentions. Ultimately, they gave her two months to choose a suitor of her preference or would decide for her. Her parents believed she was overdue for marriage and saw no reason why she wasn't at her age. There were a bunch of eligible guys asking for her hand in marriage. Bintou was afraid that her parents had someone already in mind, and that was why they were in such a hurry.

Aliou sent two letters that week, one to Bintou to soothe her fears. Although he was scared; trying his best to persuade her he would never allow something like that to happen. The second letter was to his father, describing the case and begging him to go meet Bintou's mother and father to express his son's interest in marrying Bintou and to help plan. Aliou knew he was putting himself inside a hot pot of soup; because the next time he would come home for the approaching break, people would ask him about the marriage. They would have already believed he was ready, due to the exalted notions they had of the capital.

About the betrothal arrangements, he was almost sure his parents wouldn't object but didn't know whether Bintou's parents would. He was the most mature suitor of the young– sters in the village, seeing that he was a small-time hero of some sort now.

Aliou waited restlessly for a response, and after a week which seemed like months, he got a reply from Bintou. Surprisingly, her parents were more than delighted to agree, but they had a condition. They wouldn't want to wait too long Aliou didn't know whether to scream or weep, so he rushed to his cousin Daouda for guidance.

Daouda had focused on what Aliou said and replied, "Whatever you do, I support you. Write them back and tell them you must complete his secondary school first. You need a steady job to take care of her and their children to come." Daouda went on to tell Aliou. These were the wisest words that he ever heard from him. Aliou then did as advised. After days of considerable persuasion from his father and tribe, Bintou's family happily agreed.

Daouda started having a drinking problem, out of sight from Aliou and his friends. Aliou suspected something but out of respect for his folk, rejected his suspicions. His people were raised in a religious community that frowned on alcohol. The night he first saw his cousin Daouda taking a sip from a bottle that resembled alcohol, he was more than shocked. As days passed by, odd jobs became scarce for Daouda. He tried to persuade Aliou and his friends to drink with him. All had declined. Life in the city was a hell but stay strong. If Aliou came back home with nothing, his village would mock him and look upon him in disappointment.

Curiousity set in on Aliou one afternoon when his cousin kept pressuring him to drink. He kept saying "Only a sip." Daouda passed him the bottle. The burning sensation and smell caused him to spit it out. Aliou vowed to never take a sip again.

At first, Daouda only drank with his friends at night. Due to the lack of work, his drinking worsened and missed opportunities to work because of his tardiness. His body frame became thinner, and he was always fussing about everything. Aliou tried advising, but it was a waste of time. Whenever Daouda was drunk, he would tell Aliou to sit close, ranting about the hardships that had occurred in his life.

"I came top in my class, but there was no money to continue my education. And now, nobody wants to employ me even though I have a good secondary school result." Daouda yelled in a drunken tone between cries and laughter." And you will hear the stupid people in our village telling their kids to be like me. Why will they be like me? They don't even know what it feels like to be me. How can they know? They have never stepped out of the village in their miserable lives. Do you know what it feels like to come first in your class and then go out to the big city to go to the same job for little money with people who had never stepped into a classroom?"

Aliou tried to help him by hiding or taking the bottles away. Sometimes, Daouda would give in and go to sleep. And other times, he would protest, insult Aliou, and take the bottle back, drinking himself to a point in which he wouldn't be able to differentiate between his left and right hand. It was breaking Aliou's heart to see Daouda losing control of himself, so he went to seek help.

He wanted to talk to Bintou about it, but he felt like he will only betray his cousin's trust by doing so. Besides, what does Bintou know about anything of that sort? She could only sympathise. One day after school, he approached Yusuf to seek his opinion. Yusuf told him he knew of a community leader that helped people to get back on the right track and gave Aliou the man's address.

The community leader had a compound dedicated to helping young people with drug and drinking problems, and he did it for free. Participants had to do minimal labour around the compound to support themselves while he kept an eye on them.

Help was there for Daouda but convincing him to go would be difficult. When Aliou brought up the topic, Daouda kept saying he was fine. Tired of it all, Aliou approached his cousin's best friend one night and explained the situation to him. Though the two friends drank together sometimes, his friend was more responsible than his cousin. He held a full- time job and was married.

Aliou and the man went to speak with Daouda, but he again denied he had a drinking problem. Daouda kept saying it was normal, and to leave him alone. The following day seemed worse when Daouda fell down the stairs in front of the house. When they saw this happen, they devised a plan to trick him into going to the man's place.

His friend begged him the next day to escort him to visit someone willing to give them a job, and Daouda agreed. The weather was nice, and the streets weren't too busy. After Daouda and his friend had left, Aliou packed Daouda's clothes into a small backpack and headed to the community leader's house. The site manager welcomed Daouda and his friend and escorted them inside as if everything was normal. A minute later, his friend had excused himself and left without Daouda noticing. A few minutes later, Daouda asked where his friend was, and it was said that he left.

He started yelling like a man defeated, trying to fight everyone in sight. The staff refused to let him leave. Daouda was tricked for his own good. Aliou came by later that evening to drop off Daouda's clothes and foodstuff. He was not permitted to see his cousin.

During the first couple weeks of treatment, Daouda refused to take visitors. Later, Aliou and his best friend came by but Daouda would refuse to acknowledge that he knew them. However, they kept visiting based on the advice of the staff.

A month into the treatment, Daouda started getting better. He was more functional and requested his cousin and best friend now come visit him. He realised that they had saved his life and acknowledged he wouldnt be alive without them. Aliou was more than happy to see Daouda getting better.

There were times when Aliou would cook and take food to him. If not, he would spend his afternoons when not work- ing; playing games and talking about school and Islam. Daouda spent over six months in the rehabilitation centre, and for the first time since being in the city, Aliou did not go back home for the holidays. He kept telling Bintou and his relatives in letters that he was studying hard for extra classes.

After Daouda was discharged, he came home a changed man, trying his best to work. He continued looking for a job that would put his secondary school certificate to good use. Daouda believed in the future, and that is what counted.

A month after his release, Daouda was very fortunate. The local government council in his village area was hiring and wanted him for the job. He would have to relocate back to the village, leaving Aliou to fend for himself in the city. It would not be a problem, Aliou assured him. By now, he was used to the city, so it didn't bother him to stay alone. There were still odd jobs at his cousin's old working places, and he could earn enough money to survive.

Three months went by, and before Aliou knew it, the school year was almost over. On most evenings if he wasn't working, he would go to the local football field to play football with the boys in the neighbourhood and made quite a reputation for himself.

The final year exams were approaching, and Aliou studied very hard. He wanted to travel home afterward. News from the village was written in a letter delivered to Daouda's friend that his father was critically ill. Daouda informed his friend that the message should not be given until after he finished the exams.

When the news reached Aliou, he quickly rushed back home and found his father in a terrible condition. The atmosphere in the house was depressing. Everyone moved around on tiptoes; scared that if they were loud, the old man would collapse and die. During the evenings, the village imam was brought to recite the Quran over his father, hoping to cure him and ward off every evil intended to harm him. His mother and the other wives took turns taking care of him and praying for him nonstop.

Two and a half weeks later, Aliou's father had passed away. His elder sister was the one who found him. The women were busy making a fire to cook breakfast, when Aliou's mother called her husband's name. Since he didn't answer, so she assumed that he was sleeping. After noticing that he slept longer than usual, Aliou's mother sent his sister to wake him up. She went over to his room, saying Ifama (dad) and touched him, only to feel that his body had gone limp and cold as ice.

She screamed immediately, alarming the rest of the people in the compound. Her mother was the first one to come in, followed by the other wives, kids, and relatives. The women wailed and rolled on the floor, with the first daughter fainting on the spot. Aliou ran to the imam's house so he could come to prepare for the burial while fighting back a lot of tears.

The imam hurried. Based on Muslim traditions, a person is buried right away, unless there are specific reasons other– wise. Neighbours soon pooled into the house, each wearing a mournful face. Aliou's father was a respectable man and was admired by the villagers. Pain floated in the air as the body was removed from the house for the washing.

People came from neighbouring villages. Women comforted the wives while crying with them. Others began preparation of food for the guests. No matter how fast a person died, food for the visitors was an essential part after the funeral. The imam, Aliou, and his brothers did the ritual bath and shrouded him in white.

It was a painful experience indeed. Later that midday, after the prayer, their father was buried in the local cemetery. Many people graced the unfortunate occasion as the imam (community religious leader) led the prayers, and it was then that Aliou's tears came gushing down his face. His father's body was lowered into the grave, and everyone made suppli– cations for him. After the burial, more visitors came to the house to offer their condolences.

It was only at night that Aliou had time to grieve in peace. He cried so hard in the middle of the night. The next morning, Aliou woke up early, performed his ablution, and prayed hard for his deceased father. His father may not be the most friendly or playful father, but he was sympathetic to the people he met and had raised several children whose parents he didn't even know. He was a good father by the village standards; giving the best life he could to his family even though he wasn't wealthy.

After days of mourning, people ceased coming to the house, while the house looked as if it had been deserted. It was something that occurred with the death of the breadwinner of any household in the community. The dwelling was dead unless someone filled that shoe which was now left to him and his brothers. Aliou knew now he had to work hard and maybe leave school.

Since Aliou and Bintou were now engaged, they could see each other. She was his strongest supporter, always knowing the right thing to say and giving him space when needed. Although her family had pestered him about the wedding, they paused for a period out of respect for his father's death. Aliou knew it was only a matter of time before they asked again.

He didn't know what to do. There was just a lot to handle. How could he balance taking care of his household and being married, with the societal expectations of weddings? It would take planning and perhaps leaving school altogether.

His cousin, Daouda was supportive by helping the family with the upkeep of the home as much as he could. Considering Aliou's dad was a father to him and had raised him after his own father had passed away, he gave as much as he could. The wonderful thing was that Daouda's job paid well.

Aliou later received a letter from Yusuf; telling him that the results of their final exams were issued. Aliou and Yusuf passed their exams with flying colours. Aliou replied explaining that he was taking care of his late father's inter– ests and will be in the capital in another month. The dilemma was that each pupil on scholarship had to enrol no later than a month after the final exams. Aliou wasn't lucky enough to get back to the city in time to renew.

His life was shattering; he didn't know what to do. There was just too much going on. "Why me?" he questioned. The scholarship was his sole hope for a prosperous future. As urged by Yusuf, Aliou came back to the capital to find a full- time job while still working at his old workplace. Nothing was too little at this point in his life.

8

ANYTHING IS POSSIBLE

Aliou went everywhere he knew he could get a job, but most of them were not hiring. And even when they were hiring, they were looking for someone with a university degree. His cousin Daouda tried to see if he could get him a job in his office close to the village, but it was all in vain. He didn't have the right connection to get Aliou in.

One evening after Aliou came home from playing football, Yusuf came to him with a dream opportunity; he told him that there was a way that could put an end to all their financial headaches. Yusuf explained, "We can take the backway out of the country and make it to Italy. There we would have a better life and send monies to our families." Aliou was sceptical at first, but Yusuf kept talking about how he knew people that had done it before. "We must do this, or we will die in Gambia with empty stomachs." Yusuf came up with a plan and told Aliou that if he agreed, they could take their monies to a smuggler to board a ship heading into Europe, which was set to leave in fifteen days. However, he explained that they would have to pay the money to someone in town beforehand and would have to stop in Libya for only a few nights. Aliou gave thought overnight to Yusuf's words and in the morning; decided that it was the only chance he had left if he wanted to marry Bintou and take care of his family.

Aliou gathered his savings and gave almost half to Yusuf. He then wrote a letter to Bintou fabricating to her about his progress in school and working status. He didn't tell her about the lack of scholarship. Aliou knew by the time their reply would reach him, he would already in Italy working. It was time to go to the market to gather things for the long journey. Aliou bought simple perishables, water, and some medicines.

The following dawn, he and Yusuf departed to the place to meet the smuggler. The smuggler was late, and as soon as he arrived, he asked for money and increased the price. Aliou shouted that they already agreed on the price for the journey. The husky man demanded more and said he was providing them VIP service on the ship. Yusuf paid the difference, and when they arrived, they saw about fifty men, women, and children waiting at the beach outside the ship. They thought they were the only ones travelling. The ship was old and only used to convey large goods in containers. The smugglers told everyone they would have to hide inside each of them.

They promised to get everyone to their destination and stressed that everyone has his or her provisions. Once each person had taken a position in the containers, the ship sailed. Aliou had never been on a boat before and felt nauseous. A man next to him vomited as soon as the motors of the ship cranked.

Aliou packed raw foodstuff, just in case he and Yusuf needed to eat a solid meal. There was no kitchen onboard, and the occupants were ordered to stay in their places for their own security.

When the ship reached an area of heavy police presence, there were navy sailors who would come aboard, briefly search the cargo and ask for bribes for permission of passage. The captain of the ship once served with the navy police, so he would give them something valuable, and they would look the other way.

The journey was a long one. Aliou, Yusuf and the

rest of the migrants had been at sea for weeks. Everyone on board became friends with one another; each telling his story. The common goal was to go to Europe to make better lives for themselves and their families.

All the passengers were from other West African countries. Aliou shared a container with a Cameroonian family; a man, his wife, and their two children. The man tried to talk to Aliou, but Aliou didn't know French or his native language. He could only nod yes or no. There were others from Mali, Togo, Niger, and Benin. Each one of them speaking his own mother-tongue when explaining his story.

As the journey entered the second month, they all soon learned the hard way they also needed to be very careful with their things. Some passengers ran out of foodstuff and were desperate to do anything to eat. They sent their kids to steal food from the other passengers' quarters in the containers. Once discovered, the father of the child would have to apologise and return the stuff. Everyone's provisions had reduced, and there was no excuse. After a week or so, and a series of events on the ship, the captain announced they had reached Libya. There was a loud yell of relief. The passengers were happy. At least, they were closer to Europe although still in Africa.

The smugglers had other plans and announced

they would take the migrants in small groups to another boat to decrease their chances of getting caught. The riders didn't care if the families stayed together and reached Italy. Aliou and Yusuf were two of the first to leave, and they were eager after being in the containers for such a long time.

A car arrived to pick them up where they were taken to a very large house in the middle of nowhere. The migrants felt it was an unusual place to go to get another ship. They stood quietly for the sake of their journey. The driver and another man went in the house after Aliou and Yusuf as the place appeared to be heavily guarded.

"Why all the security just to get on the ship?" asked Aliou in the little Arabic he knew.

A smuggler understood him and responded, Ma fee Muskilah (It's not a problem). "Ijlas" (Sit down). Aliou, Yusuf and a few others sat quietly on the chairs assuming that they would board the boat soon.

The smugglers' friendly and open tones changed totally from there on out. They became harsh and intimidating when Aliou and Yusuf kept asking them when they were leaving. The pirates then drove the two to another area where other men were squatting and turning lifelessly in an unfurnished room. Most appeared battered as though they were struck with something heavy. It was at that moment that

Aliou and Yusuf realised that the smugglers were not going to take them to Europe and had their own plans.

Aliou and Yusuf perceived they were in great trouble. They couldn't give up without a fight, so they fought. Unfortunately, all the men were either stocky or fat with beards, and all were armed with pistols. They overpowered Aliou and Yusuf with ease. One of them hit Aliou with something heavy from behind, and he fainted.

When Aliou woke up, he realised that one of his hands was chained to a pole. The light was too bright for his eyes as he first opened them, but he slowly adjusted his sight to his surroundings. He looked around and saw Yusuf shackled to another beam and unconscious." Yusuf, Yusuf." Aliou shouted. He was too far to reach him. Aliou felt tears burn his eyelids and regretted his decision to leave home. It was all too late to wish now.

He then heard sobbing beside him and turned to look at the Cameroonian man that had shared a container with him, crying.

"They took them away! I don't know where they took them. My wife and kids were screaming and crying, but I could do nothing to save them. I must protect them, but I have failed them as a father."

He broke down as he described his struggles with the built thugs. The Cameroonian and his family were taken from the ship's location a day after Aliou and Yusuf and was split up by the bandits in headbands.

Aliou wanted to comfort the man, but he couldn't speak his tongue. He was at a loss for words as he imagined what he would have felt if Bintou was taken away from him in that manner. Aliou was grateful he wasn't married in his present crises.

"I am sorry," he told the Cameroonian in English and genuinely meant it.

But Aliou shouldn't be the one to apologise.

"The pirates were at fault for tearing the man away from his family. The Westerners are responsible for their wrong choices in invading this place; disrupting its peace and security. The government was at fault for failing to unify the country and maintaining stability."

All thoughts which pounced around in Aliou's mind as he watched the Cameroonian. His heart bled for the man who so obviously loved his family so much. Even on the ship, the man was always around making sure his family were as comfortable as they could get.

"All I wanted to do was give them a better life. And now I have lost them," the man continued.

Aliou tried to remind him that it was not his fault but couldn't. He looked back when his father had died, and the way he felt like beating the people coming with their assurances of foresight. The Cameroonian may have to come to terms that he may never see his family again.He wished the man's pain would simply vanish. The only thing that Aliou could do is say these words in Arabic "Hasbunallah wa Na'mal Wakeel" (Suffice is Allah and he is the best of disposers of affairs) at that point. There was nothing anyone could do except supplicate for relief.

After what seemed like ages, Yusuf regained consciousness.

"Aliou... Aliou... I am so sorry! I'm sorry... I didn't know. If I have had known, I wouldn't have made you come." He kept apologising.

"It's not your fault." Deep down, a part of him felt angry, partly blaming Yusuf for all that had transpired. Aliou knewYusuf was as much as a victim as himself.

Aliou felt anger flow through his veins, an amount of anger that he had never felt before. He wanted to hit and destroy something. Specifically, the heads of the dealers. But this was his fate now. Aliou kept thinking about home, wondering what would come of his mother if he never went back home. What about Bintou? Would she move on without him? Will they all think he had abandoned them? What about the entire family that his father had left behind? What about his siblings who placed so much hope on him?

With those depressing thoughts weighing down his mind. Aliou fell asleep and woke up abruptly when food was brought to the room.

"Yallah! Yallah!" the men hollered telling everyone in the room to get up.

No one communicated with each other; each absorbed in his own thoughts; thinking about what was and what would be. They all sat up, eating couscous and meat that was put in front of them like prisoners of war in captivity. The prisoners wished they had known about the horrors that awaited them, perhaps they would have stayed wherever it was that they were in the first place. Yusuf refused to eat and was hit with the butt of a pistol across the head. "Kul aw Maut" (Eat or die!) He knew then started eating as well.

All the dreams of going to Europe had now been crushed before their very own eyes. Suddenly during the night, some guards ran in and ordered everyone all out. Aliou and the rest were taken down a long corridor and then moved into a larger room where a few black and Arab men were seated. One guard announced that the prisoners would each be given a raqam (number), and whoever hears his number must stand in front or else he will be executed. Aliou and Yusuf understood the Arabs because they learned Arabic in Dara (Islamic schools for young people). The other hostages struggled to figure out what the gunmen were doing and were terrified.

Aliou's number was five and it was called to step forward. The gunmen examined him some type of bush animal, searching his buttocks and teeth.

"Why are they doing this?" Aliou thought.

He had once saw a film in school about slavery. But Aliou wondered what the gunmen would do if anyone protested or wasn't chosen? After he was checked out by the pirates, the other captives, fortunately, had their numbers called. All were made to remain in the front line with Aliou; waiting to hear what would happen next. Each of them wondering is this the end. The dealers and gunmen seemed to be negotiating for a while and kept screaming at one another in Arabic what suggested that it was about the price of each captive. All of them began choosing whom that they demanded as slaves. Aliou was taken early. Unfortunately, Aliou was barely given enough time to say goodbye to Yusuf, and they both cried hard while separated. Not knowing if they would ever see one another again, Aliou and Yusuf tried to fight the captors to no avail. Aliou was forced into the back of the truck with some others into the midst of the remaining moonlight.

In the midst of the night, the vehicle treaded the deserted sandy roads until they reached a place like the first one, only that it was a bit smaller. There were many people inside; most were Blacks who looked exhausted while working. All stopped what they were doing for a second to give Aliou looks that held so much sadness, and from their eyes, he could see the pain in their souls. They did not know Aliou, and what his fate would be, however, they seemed to be mourning for him.

He was taken to a room upstairs. The room was moderate, there were two bunk beds with no mattresses. Two men were in the room. Both were African, but Aliou realised they were not Gambians. They didn't resemble his countrymen's features. With no speech or explanation of what was going on, the bandits locked the door behind and walked away.

"You are here for the fight?" One man, short in stature and chubby asked him in Arabic.

"A fight? What fight?" Aliou said defensively in Arabic confused by the man's question. "No one had said anything about any fight. What kind of fight were they even talking about?"

The other taller and darker man sighed. He looked older and had a strong-looking physique. He spoke English which was a sign of relief for Aliou and said, "They brought us here to fight. I can see why they chose you. You are young and strong. These Arabs pay huge sums of money just to gather around and watch us poor black people fight and kill ourselves like animals." His words revealed pain and disgust." The worst part was that it was our fellow black brothers who sold us to the Arabs."

Aliou felt his head spinning. What were they talking about? He didn't know how to fight? Was this how his life would end? Killed in a strange country, fighting men to the death? What kind of life was that? His tears poured as the reality set in that he may never see his family again.

"Look! Cheer up..." The short man said "It is not a fight to the death." He pointed to a scar on his shoulders. The wound looked so painful that Aliou winced. An hour later, the dealers came to room hastily saying Yallah (Let's go). Aliou looked around innocently as he lined up being led to perhaps his death.

The first fight was tough and bloody. He beat the man to a gory pulp after taking many shots and had to spend a few days recovering. After one maid said he was healthy enough to fight again, Aliou was forced to fight once a day sometimes in duels. The Africans fought one another as if they were enemies. These militias would hold tournaments and bring their best slave fighters and gamble on the winner. Somehow, Aliou was blessed to survive. At the end of each fight night, Aliou wondered whatever happened to Yusuf and prayed to Allah to leave this place for good.

After a few months of fighting, his prayers were answered. The Africans in the house began rallying in the midst of the night and plotted a rebellion. The plan would be that one guard help them get the basement keys. One man, who was responsible for cleaning the kitchen, would start a fire in the basement around midnight drawing the Arabs and then locking them inside. The middle of the night was the best time because most of the militia went home and came back the next morning before the captives were awaken. There were four Arab militiamen on watch that night, outside smoking cigarettes and listening to the radio when the fire had broken out. When they smelled the smoke, they all ran to the basement and were locked inside; burning to death.

The Africans freed all the captives in the house and were told to run away. Two men running beside Aliou; Ibrahim and Musa, were the masterminds. A group of eight made their way through the night on foot. The guard who helped them escape was half-African. His pity for them would not go unrewarded as everyone thanked him for helping them. All hoped to leave Libya before the Arabs found out what happened. Aliou preferred to go back home, but the closest boat leaving on the rendezvous was headed for Italy according to the guardsman. All the men were adamant about getting on another boat, but little choice did they have at that point. It was escape or die.

After a few hours on foot into the deep sands of the Sahara, they arrived at the shore. Aliou wanted to leave this terrible place. He tried asking around for Yusuf in the words of Arabic 'Ayna Sadeeqi meaning where is my friend?'. The Cameroonian, who escaped, waved his hands to signal that Yusuf was sold off to some unknown militia in another part of the country. He was reluctant to leave his family behind in Libya, so he didn't board. Aliou wept for his friend Yusuf and raised his hands to Allah to ask him for his safety. The smugglers hurried up everyone else to escape the gleaming light of daybreak. Yusuf would never be forgotten.

Most of the men's wounds were worsening and

three out of seven had passed away. Aliou kept experiencing stomach pains; resulting from the blows in the fights. Day by day, the pains seemed to grow worse.

Headed to Italy in a journey that would take another four weeks, Aliou fell terribly weak at sea. And a week before the ship arrived, he sensed he wouldn't make it, although Ibrahim and Musa tried to make him believe otherwise. His soul was slowly fading away. He requested a pen and paper and wrote three letters; one addressed to the love of his life, Bintou, telling her how much he loved her and how he wished for nothing more than her happiness. He'd ended the letter with: "Keep smiling my love, and even if I am not there to see it, know it will be enough for me no matter where I am. If you are reading this letter, then know I am where nothing but your prayers can reach me.

"I love you Bintou, be happy for me."

The second letter was addressed to his sister, telling her how much she means to him, and he ended the letter with: "This is for you and Ummi (mama). Tell her that her son will forever remember her love. And even if she cannot read this, I hope she will feel the impact of these words. Be happy now."

The last letter was addressed to Daouda, it was more of a letter of appreciation and a plea to take care of his family. He ended with the words:

"For all the times you made me chase the greatness within me, I am forever grateful. But please, I ask for one last favour; please hold dear and care for the family I left behind. I wish you all the best."

A year later, Bintou received the letter Aliou had sent her through Ibrahim and Musa. They made it to Italy and were at a refugee-processing center trying to get their immigration papers. Her hands shook while reading it, for she could feel Aliou everywhere in that letter. Her tears fell on the paper, mixing with the dried ones he had left behind; the letters were supposed to be sent by Aliou and not for him. The love of her life had died at the tender age of nineteen.

After Aliou's sister read her letter, she grieved, hiding her tears. She proceeded to her mother's room to read aloud to their mother translating into the local language what had become of her beloved son; the first words caused her to faint. She grieved for her son for weeks who was buried at sea in a place unknown. Everyone in the village wondered what made Aliou do this? Was it Daouda? Was it Bintou pushing him for the marriage? No one had the answers.

Daouda owed everything he had to the cousin

whose life he had failed in need of help. Aliou had saved him, and Daouda forever felt in debt to his beloved cousin. After four months of receiving the Aliou's letter, Daouda and Bintou married out of respect of Aliou. No one knew the mercy of Allah. The village would always tell stories of their beloved son, and his face would be forever remembered.

AFTERWORD

As migration to Western countries are at an all-time high, I hope that this book will shed light on the need of both migrating and recipient countries of addressing the issue even further. Many have died including women and children going the Backway but those who have survived to share their tales have often be in fear about their ordeals due to family backlash or fear of deportation.

We kindly ask that you consider reviewing the book and reading our other titles.

www.ingramcontent.com/pod-product-compliance
Lightning Source LLC
Chambersburg PA
CBHW031031190726
48286CB00003BA/1118

9781925988260